# MUD!

by Wendy Cheyette Lewison
Illustrated by Bill Basso

**Hello Reader!—Level 1**

SCHOLASTIC INC.
New York   Toronto   London   Auckland   Sydney
Mexico City   New Delhi   Hong Kong

## Hello, Family Members,

Learning to read is one of the most important accomplishments of early childhood. **Hello Reader!** books are designed to help children become skilled readers who like to read. Beginning readers learn to read by remembering frequently used words like "the," "is," and "and"; by using phonics skills to decode new words; and by interpreting picture and text clues. These books provide both the stories children enjoy and the structure they need to read fluently and independently. Here are suggestions for helping your child *before*, *during*, and *after* reading:

### Before
• Look at the cover and pictures and have your child predict what the story is about.
• Read the story to your child.
• Encourage your child to chime in with familiar words and phrases.
• Echo read with your child by reading a line first and having your child read it after you do.

### During
• Have your child think about a word he or she does not recognize right away. Provide hints such as "Let's see if we know the sounds" and "Have we read other words like this one?"
• Encourage your child to use phonics skills to sound out new words.
• Provide the word for your child when more assistance is needed so that he or she does not struggle and the experience of reading with you is a positive one.
• Encourage your child to have fun by reading with a lot of expression . . . like an actor!

### After
• Have your child keep lists of interesting and favorite words.
• Encourage your child to read the books over and over again. Have him or her read to brothers, sisters, grandparents, and even teddy bears. Repeated readings develop confidence in young readers.
• Talk about the stories. Ask and answer questions. Share ideas about the funniest and most interesting characters and events in the stories.

I do hope that you and your child enjoy this book.

—Francie Alexander
    Reading Specialist,
    Scholastic's Learning Ventures

ISBN 0-439-17932-7

Text copyright © 1990 by Wendy Cheyette Lewison. Illustrations copyright © 2001 by Bill Basso.
All rights reserved. Published by Scholastic Inc. SCHOLASTIC, HELLO READER, CARTWHEEL BOOKS
and associated logos are trademarks and/or registered trademarks of Scholastic Inc.

Library of Congress Cataloging-in-Publication Data
Lewison, Wendy Cheyette.
    Mud! / by Wendy Cheyette Lewison ; illustrated by Bill Basso.
        p.  cm.— (Hello reader! Level 1)
    "Cartwheel books"
    Summary: Kids having fun with mud find it on their hands and toes, in their hair, over there,
over here, and everywhere.
    ISBN 0-439-17932-7
    [1. Mud—Fiction.  2. Play—Fiction.  3. Stories in rhyme.]  I. Basso, Bill, ill.  II. Title.  III. Series.
PZ8.3.L592 Mu 2001
[E]—dc21                                                                              00-035815
30 29 28 27 26 25 24                                                    11 12 13 14 15/0

Printed in the U.S.A.     40
First printing, April 2001

For my wonderful nieces, nephews,
and grand-niece, Casey Ann.
Each one an inspiration.
– Uncle Bill

# Mud in the puddle.

# Mud on the shoe.

Mud on the socks.

# Mud on you!

# Mud on your hands.

# Mud on your toes.

# Mud on your cheeks.

# Mud on your nose.

# Mud, mud everywhere!

# Mud on your elbows.

Mud in your hair.

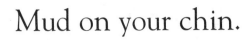

Mud on your chin.

Mud on your ear.

Mud over there.

Mud over here.

Mud in the puddle.

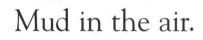

Mud in the air.

Mud, mud everywhere!

Mud!